Don't Forget Winona

by JEANNE WHITEHOUSE PETERSON

illustrated by KIMBERLY BULCKEN ROOT

JOANNA COTLER BOOKS

An Imprint of HarperCollinsPublishers

Page 12 : Two lines excerpted from "Cleano." Words and music by Woody Guthrie TRO—
Copyright 1954 (renewed) and 1963 (renewed) by Folkways Music Publishers, Inc., New York, NY.

Don't Forget Winona   Text copyright © 2004 by Jeanne Whitehouse   Illustrations copyright © 2004 by Kimberly Bulcken Root
Manufactured in China by South China Printing Company Ltd.   All rights reserved.   www.harperchildrens.com   Library of Congress
Cataloging in-Publication-Data   Peterson, Jeanne Whitehouse.   Don't forget Winona / by Jeanne Whitehouse Peterson ; illustrated by
Kimberly Bulcken Root.   p.   cm.   Summary : A young girl describes her family's experiences—
and her younger sister's antics—when a drought forces them to make their way on Route 66 from Oklahoma to California.
ISBN 0-06-027198-1 (lib. bdg.).—ISBN 0-06-027197-3   [1. Droughts—Great Plains—Fiction.   2. Sisters—Fiction.   3. Family life—
Oklahoma—Fiction.   4. Oklahoma—Fiction.]   I. Root, Kimberly Bulcken, ill.   II. Title.   PZ7.P444Do   2004   99-27255
Typography by Alicia Mikles   1   2   3   4   5   6   7   8   9   10   ❖   First Edition

For my husband, David—
for the stories we tell
and the songs we sing
traveling together
on the old highway.
—J.W.P.

For the Rev. Paul Kreyling and
Mrs. Carol Kreyling, with love
—K.B.R.

My sister's name is Winona.
She likes to laugh.
She likes to sing.
But sometimes she runs around
like a chick in a dust storm.
And she never listens—
not to me.

Ma says it's my job to watch her.
Pa's busy fixing the truck,
and Ma has Teddy-Boy to feed.
"Keep her with you, now!"
Ma always tells me.

But on the day we left Oklahoma,
my sister hid from me.
I couldn't find her in the toolshed.
She wasn't behind the old oak tree
or down by the dry creek bed.
Finally, when I looked in the back
of the truck, I found Winona between
the cook pots and the blankets.
She was laughing: "Don't forget me!"

I didn't want to sit in back with Winona,
but there was no room in front.
So we had to squeeze together.
"I'm a broom," Winona told me.
"You're a mop!"

Suddenly Pa started the engine.
I felt a *chug, chug* rumble
from my toes to my cheeks.
We were leaving our farm
because of the wind and the dust storms.
We were heading toward Route 66.

Janey chased us to the highway.
"Good-bye!" I shouted until she was out of sight.
Winona waved her kerchief and called:
"Good-bye, cat!
Good-bye, swing!
Don't forget me!"

All the way through Oklahoma,
the wind blew dust in our eyes and mouths.
We could barely breathe,
and we were always thirsty.
Sometimes we found water to drink
along the road, but sometimes it was too dirty.
Then I'd bite my lip, and Winona
would suck the tip of her finger.

When we stopped for gas in Amarillo, Texas,
Winona started to fuss:
    "I need some pop!
        Orange! Not red! Not green!"
Pa just shook his head. "There's no money."
Winona's face got all scrunched up.
"Don't cry," I said. Then I asked
the man at the filling station
for a piece of chipped ice.
Winona finally smiled.

When we stopped, Winona
was the first one out of the truck
and the first one to climb back in.
She liked throwing stones on the road
with the other kids and helping Ma
wash Teddy-Boy's dirty cheeks.
Together they sang:

"*Ma-ma, oh Ma-ma, come wash my face . . .
and make me nice and clean-o.*"

But when we crossed the New Mexico state line,
Winona was tired of riding.
"I'm too hot!" she cried. "I itch!"
"Rest with Teddy-Boy," Ma told her.
"Stay in the shade," I said.
"No!" Winona shouted. "I'm not a baby!"

Ma thought Winona was with me
under the bridge.
I thought she was with Teddy-Boy
on the front seat.
That's why I didn't look for her
when I heard the *chug, chug* rumble
of our truck. I just climbed in back.

Partway down the highway, we heard
honking and shouting.
Behind us came a truck driver
hauling broomcorn and one freckle-faced kid.
"Oh no!" Pa cried. "We forgot Winona!"

For the rest of the day Winona
leaned on my shoulder and held my hand.
By the time we got to Tucumcari,
Winona's fingers were hot.
She would not eat anything, not even
the peach pie a girl brought from town
for us Okies.
She cried in the night, then slept
through the mountains all the way
to Albuquerque.

Later, when we rested in the shade
of a cottonwood tree,
I begged Winona to open her eyes.
"Winona," I said. "Wave to that boy
on a burro. Race me to the Rio Grande.
Look!" I insisted. "A roadrunner!"
"She's sick," Ma whispered. "Let her be."

But Winona grabbed my hand.
"Don't leave!" she cried.
So I sang her a song about a cat
named Tom,
    ". . . and his tail grew long,
    and his tail grew long,
    all the way
    through Oklahoma."

Winona slept again and did not see
the coyote running across the highway.
She missed the Indian village
built on top of golden stones.
Finally, when we stopped
to fix a flat tire,
Winona sat up.
"Where's Oklahoma?" she asked.
We all laughed.
"We're a long way from
Oklahoma," Pa said.

After we crossed the Continental Divide
and followed the railroad tracks
to Gallup, Pa found a filling station
with free gas.
"This will get you to Arizona," the man said.
"You can get more in places like Holbrook,
Winslow, Winona, Flagstaff . . ."
"Winona!" Pa shouted. "You hear that?
There's a town in Arizona with my
little girl's name."

We all watched and waited to see
the signs for Winona.
It was just a tiny mountain camp,
but my sister bragged to everyone we met:
"I have a town with my very own name!"

The next day we came to a desert.
"It's so hot," Pa said, "we must cross
in the night."
After that, we climbed
a very high mountain
and only broke down twice.
Each time we stopped, we met new friends—
Okies just like us
who left home because
of the wind and the dust.

At last we looked down
on a sea-green valley.
We hugged each other until tears
filled our eyes.
"We made it!" Ma said. "This is California!"
Pa said, "We'll pick oranges in winter
and strawberries in spring."
Teddy-Boy bounced and squealed.
Winona grabbed my hand, shouting,
"Don't forget me!"
I gave my sister's fingers a squeeze.
No one could ever forget Winona.

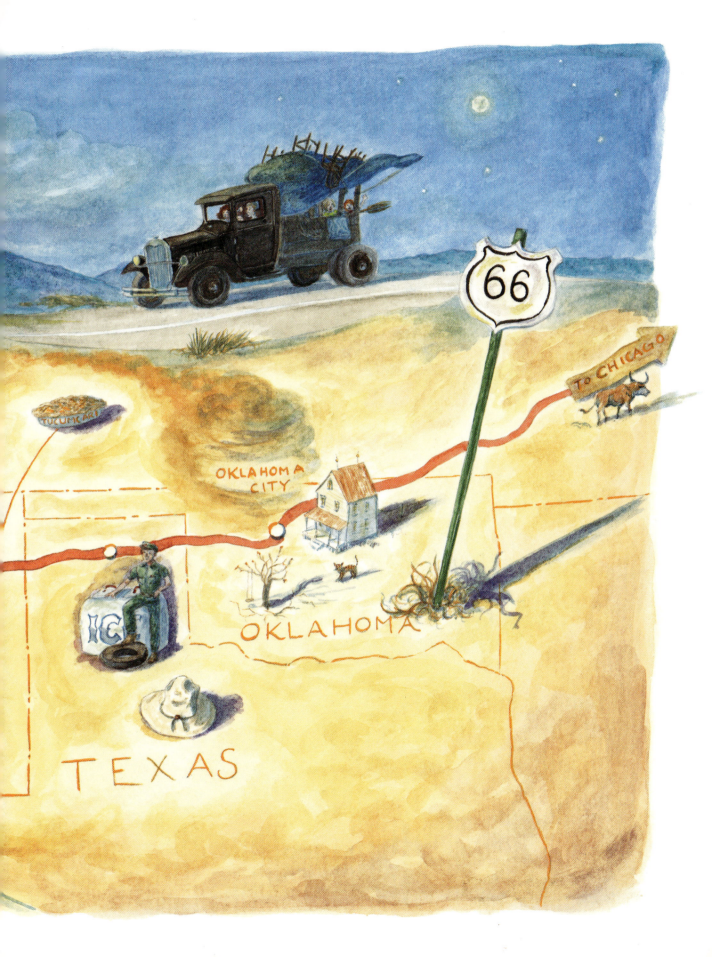

AUTHOR'S NOTE

Like Ma, Pa, Teddy-Boy, Winona, and Sarah, thousands of "Okies" moved west from Oklahoma in the late 1930s. The United States was still going through the Great Depression, and the Great Plains had come to be called the Dust Bowl since the land was so dry that dirt-filled storms whipped through the air and few crops could grow. Fortunately, used cars were cheap. So migrants piled mattresses, pans, children, and friends in the backs of old cars and trucks and began their slow journeys to a land of hope and dreams—to California.

For many, the road that took them there was Route 66. Born in 1926, Route 66 was different from other highways that stretched in straight lines from north to south, or east to west, across the continent.

Route 66 curved from Chicago, Illinois, through Missouri, Kansas, Oklahoma, Texas, New Mexico, and Arizona, all the way to Los Angeles, California. By 1937, when *Don't Forget Winona* takes place, people began to call Route 66 "America's Main Street" and "The Mother Road." All along the way travelers saw things they would never forget. For some, it was the first time they ever met people who spoke Spanish, Navajo, or Pueblo languages. For others, this was the first chance they had to drive through mountains and deserts.

In 1985, Route 66 was decommissioned. It lost its name, and all of its black-and-white Route 66 signs were taken away. But historians and members of local Route 66 associations would not let the old road die. New "Historic Route 66" signs were placed along the highway, and its seventy-fifth birthday was celebrated in 2001. More information about Route 66 is available in the library and on the Internet, where travelers from "down the road" and from as far away as Germany and Japan share stories of traveling Route 66.

—J.W.P